ESCAPE FROM

ALCATRAZ

TERROR
WOODS

BY MICHAEL DAHL

ILLUSTRATED BY PATRICIO CLAREY

raintree

a Capstone company — publishers for children

Raintree is an imprint of Capstone Global Library Limited, a company
incorporated in England and Wales having its registered office at 264
Banbury Road, Oxford, OX2 7DY – Registered company number:
6695582

www.raintree.co.uk
myorders@raintree.co.uk

Edited by Aaron J. Sautter
Designed by Kay Fraser
Original illustrations © Capstone Global Library Limited 2021
Production by Tori Abraham
Originated by Capstone Global Library Ltd

978 1 4747 9323 0

British Library Cataloguing in Publication Data
A full catalogue record for this book is available from the British Library.

Acknowledgements
Design elements: Shutterstock: Agustina Camilion, A-Star, Dima Zel,
Draw_Wing_Zen, Hybrid_Graphics, Metallic Citizen

Printed and bound in India.

CONTENTS

ERRO

PLATEAU of LENG

PHANTOM FOREST

POISON SEA

VULCAN MOUNTAINS

METAL MOON

LAKE of GOLD

DIAMOND MINES

MONSTER ZOO

PITS OF NO RETURN

PRISON STRONGHOLDS

SWAMP OF FLAME

SCARLET JUNGLE

PRISON ENERGY DRIVES

SPACE PORT PRISONER INTAKE

ABYSS OF GIANTS

ZAK

THE PRISONERS

ZAK NINE

Zak is a teenage boy from Earth Base Zeta. He dreams of piloting a star fighter one day. Zak is very brave and is a quick thinker. But his enthusiasm often leads him into trouble.

ERRO

Erro is a teenage furling from the planet Quom. He has the fur, long tail, sharp eyes and claws of his species. Erro is often impatient with Zak's reckless ways. But he shares his friend's love of adventure.

THE PRISON PLANET

Alcatraz . . . there is no escape from this terrifying prison planet. It's filled with dungeons, traps, endless deserts and other dangers. Zak Nine and his alien friend, Erro, are trapped here. They had sneaked onto a ship hoping to see an awesome space battle. But the ship landed on Alcatraz instead. Now they have to work together if they ever hope to escape!

ERRO'S STORY . . . THE PHANTOM FOREST >>>

Yesterday Zak and I were almost dinner for some meat-eating lily pads. We were lucky to escape. We need to rest, but the Alcatraz guards are following us. I believe the Phantom Forest is ahead of us. It sounds dangerous, but maybe we can hide in those dark woods . . . >>>>

CHAPTER ONE:
GIANT TREES

"Careful! It is a long way down!" I say. "You do not want to fall here."

The trees here rise hundreds of metres above the ground. Their black branches are tipped with huge, thorny leaves. We must be careful. The thorns can rip our clothes and cut us.

Zak and I are walking on a long branch. It is easier to hide from the Alcatraz guards up here.

It is also easier to avoid the huge, bloodthirsty rats below.

"This branch really is wobbly," Zak says nervously.

"Do not bounce so much!" I tell my human friend.

"I'm not bouncing," Zak says. "You're the one bouncing!"

Each time the branch wobbles, the thorny leaves shake.

shhk-shhk, shhk-shhk

"Shh! Don't make so much noise!" hisses Zak. "The guards might hear us."

I want to say that *he* is making the leaves shake. Zak is wearing boots. He is having trouble moving on the branches.

He is not lucky like me. My feet have strong claws that grip the branch.

zzz-JINK! . . . zzz-JINK! . . . zzz-JINK! . . .

"Those leaves are driving me nuts!" says Zak.

"It is not the leaves," I tell him. "Something else is making that sound."

CHAPTER TWO:
SPIDER JAWS

SSSSSSSSSSSSSSS!

Now something is hissing behind Zak. He stops and slowly turns around. Then we see it. A huge spider is climbing onto our branch.

"Ugh!" Zak grunts. "That thing is gross!"

Black hairs on its body wiggle as if they are alive. Slimy green drool drips from its wicked jaws.

The spider stops and stares with its
nine glowing eyes. Then the eyes begin
blinking on and off.

"What is going on?" I say.

The spider's jaws open wide. Then it
speaks in an electronic voice.

"Give yourselves up! We are below you. We can track your every move!"

"It's the guards!" says Zak.
"That spider thing is a robot tracker."

The robot spider's sharp metal jaws snap open and shut. Its spiky legs creep along the branch towards us.

"We will have to jump," I tell Zak.

"Jump where?" he asks.

I see another thick branch nearby.

"There!" I cry out, and then I jump.

CHAPTER THREE

THE WRONG BRANCH

The branch's slippery bark is hard to grip. So I sit with my legs on either side of it.

Zak jumps and lands in front of me. He falls forward and hugs the branch tight.

"This branch wobbles too," says
Zak. "But at least we got away from
that spider-bot."

"This branch is not just wobbling," I say. "It is moving!"

The branch starts to curve in front of Zak. It keeps curving until it forms a circle around us.

SSS-SSS-SSS-SSS-SSS-SSS!

Suddenly a long, red tongue darts above my head. Then I notice the black wings growing from the bark.

We are not on a tree branch. We are sitting on the back of a flying serpent!

CHAPTER FOUR

THE SERPENT SCREAMS

The serpent's head rises above us. It stares first at Zak and then at me.

"That thing probably hasn't seen anything like us before," says Zak.

"Grab on. Whatever happens, do not let go," I tell Zak. "I cannot see the ground from up here."

SSS-SSS-SSS-SSS-SSS-SSS!

The serpent twists, turns and jerks violently.

Suddenly, Zak loses his grip. I reach out to grab his hand. But he is thrown off the beast before I can reach him! I watch helplessly as he falls.

"Aaaahhhhhhhh!" Zak screams. Then silence.

Zak has disappeared into the gloom of the forest.

The serpent jerks again, but I dig
my claws into the creature's wings.
The serpent shrieks in pain.

SSSSKKRRRAAAAAAGGKK!!

Then I hear a faint voice from below.

"Erro, my coat caught on a branch," Zak says. "I'm bleeding, but I'm okay."

I am happy to hear my friend's voice. But then the serpent flies down towards Zak.

"It is coming after you!" I shout.

CHAPTER FIVE:
SNATCHED!

I hold tightly to the serpent's wings.
I duck and dodge thorny leaves as we
fly between tree branches.

I can see Zak! He waves to me.

The serpent dives steeply down to
him. I slide down its long body towards
the head.

I dig in my claws to stop sliding.

SSSSKKRRRAAAAAWWWW!!

The serpent roars again and suddenly stops in mid-air.